GOVERNMENT IN Australia

Nicolas Brasch

Australia • Brazil • Japan • Korea • Mexico • Singapore • Spain • United Kingdom • United States

Government in Australia

Fast Forward
Turquoise Level 17

Text: Nicolas Brasch
Editor: Cameron Macintosh
Design: Stella Vassiliou
Series design: James Lowe
Production controller: Seona Galbally
Photo research: Michelle Cottrill
Audio recordings: Juliet Hill, Picture Start
Spoken by: Matthew King and Abbe Holmes

Acknowledgements
The author and publisher would like to acknowledge permission to reproduce material from the following sources: Photographs by Photographs by AAP Image/ Alan Porritt, p7/Lee Jin-man, p14 bottom/ Paul Miller, p 20 bottom; Fairfax Photos/Chris Lane, p10/ Eddie Jim, p20 top/Jason South, p19 bottom Joe Armao, p23/Kate Geraghty, p16 top/ Rebecca Hallas, p15/ Robert Pearce, p19 top/Robert Rough, p17 top; Getty Images/Ian Waldie, back cover, p16 bottom; National Archives of Australia, A1200, L13366A, pp 8-9; Newsphotos, front cover right, pp 1 right, 6/ Chris Eastman, pp 21 top, 22/ Robert Pozo, p 11 bottom; Newspix/David Smith, pp 22 -23/David Sproule, p4/ Emily Butler, p21 bottom/ Graham Crouch, p14 top/ John Feder, front cover left, pp 1 left, 13/Marc McCormack, p18/ Michael Potter, p11 top/Ray Strange, p12; Photolibrary/Bob Winsett, p17 bottom; Thomson Learning Australia/Michelle Cottrill, p5.

ISBN 978 0 17 012626 7
ISBN 978 0 17 012621 2 (set)

Cengage Learning Australia
Level 7, 80 Dorcas Street
South Melbourne, Victoria Australia 3205
Phone: 1300 790 853

Cengage Learning New Zealand
Unit 4B Rosedale Office Park
331 Rosedale Road, Albany, North Shore NZ 0632
Phone: 0800 449 725

For learning solutions, visit **cengage.com.au**

Printed in Australia by Ligare Pty Ltd
7 8 9 10 11 12 13 20 19 18 17 16

THE UNIVERSITY OF MELBOURNE

Evaluated in independent research by staff from the Department of Language, Literacy and Arts Education at the University of Melbourne.

GOVERNMENT IN Australia

Nicolas Brasch

Contents

Chapter 1	**Government**	4
Chapter 2	**The Australian System of Government**	8
Chapter 3	**Australia's Federal Parliament**	12
Chapter 4	**State and Territory Parliaments**	18
Chapter 5	**Local Governments**	22
Glossary and Index		24

GOVERNMENT

A government is a group of people
who make decisions about the way people live.
Governments make decisions
about what people can and can't do.

Governments also make decisions about how a country, state or community runs.

Governments are elected by the people they represent. People vote for the person they want to represent them in parliament.

Australia's federal parliament

Parliament is the body that is made up of all the **representatives** who are successful at an election.

Chapter 2

THE AUSTRALIAN SYSTEM OF GOVERNMENT

Australia's system of government is known as a federal system. Countries with federal systems were once made up of different states with their own governments.

At some point, the state governments handed over some of their powers to a government that would make decisions for all of them.

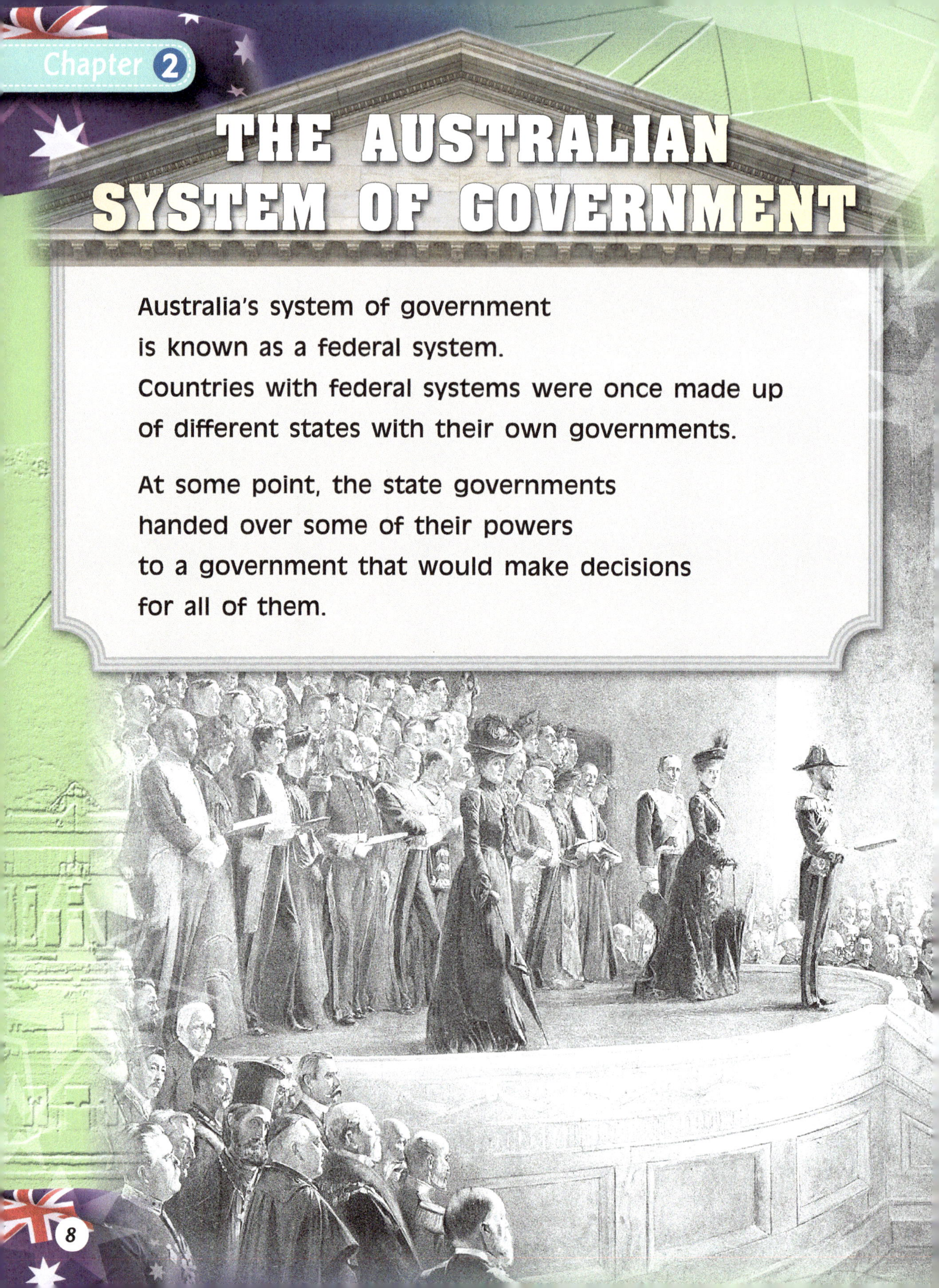

Australia's first federal government was formed in Melbourne in 1901.

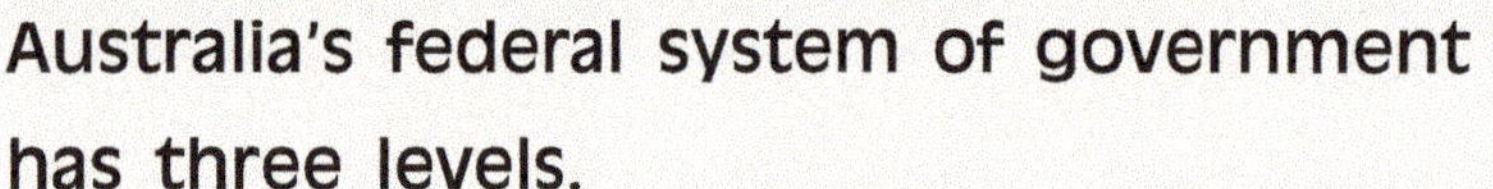

Australia's federal system of government has three levels.

The first level is the Australian, or federal parliament. It makes decisions for the whole of Australia.

At the second level are the state and **territory** parliaments. These parliaments make decisions for their own state or territory.

The third level is local government. Local governments make decisions for local communities.

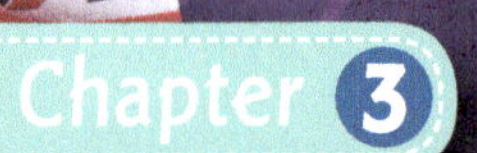

AUSTRALIA'S FEDERAL PARLIAMENT

Australia's federal parliament has two houses – a lower house and an upper house.

The lower house is called the House of Representatives. The role of the House of Representatives is to introduce laws.

The House of Representatives is also known as the seat of the government. The political party that has the most representatives in the House of Representatives forms the government.

The upper house is called the Senate.
The role of the Senate is to **review** the laws introduced in the House of Representatives.

The federal parliament is responsible for areas of life that affect all Australians,
such as customs and immigration,
defence, foreign affairs and telecommunications.

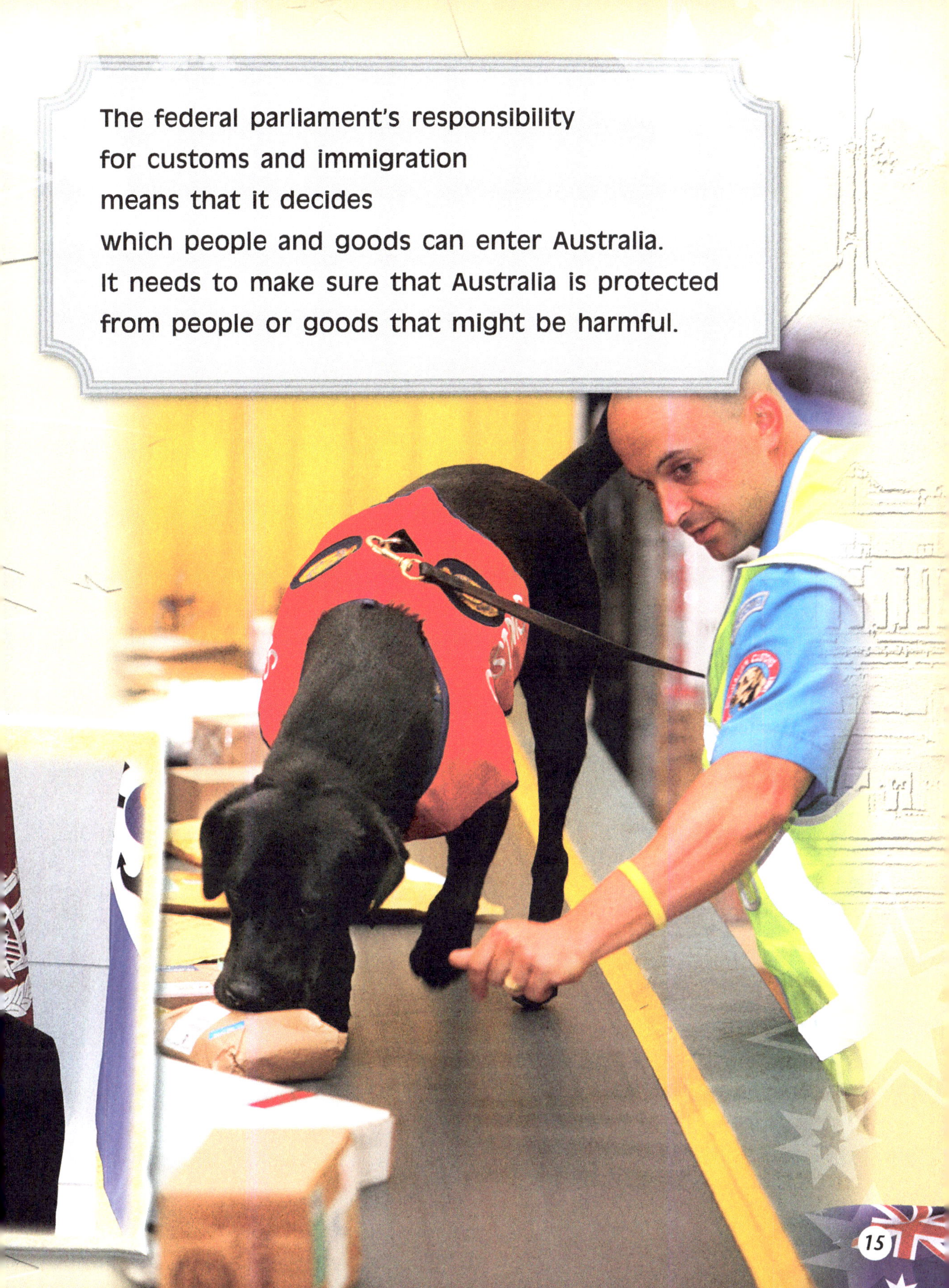

The federal parliament's responsibility for customs and immigration means that it decides which people and goods can enter Australia. It needs to make sure that Australia is protected from people or goods that might be harmful.

The federal parliament's responsibility for defence means that it is in charge of protecting Australia and its people from other countries.

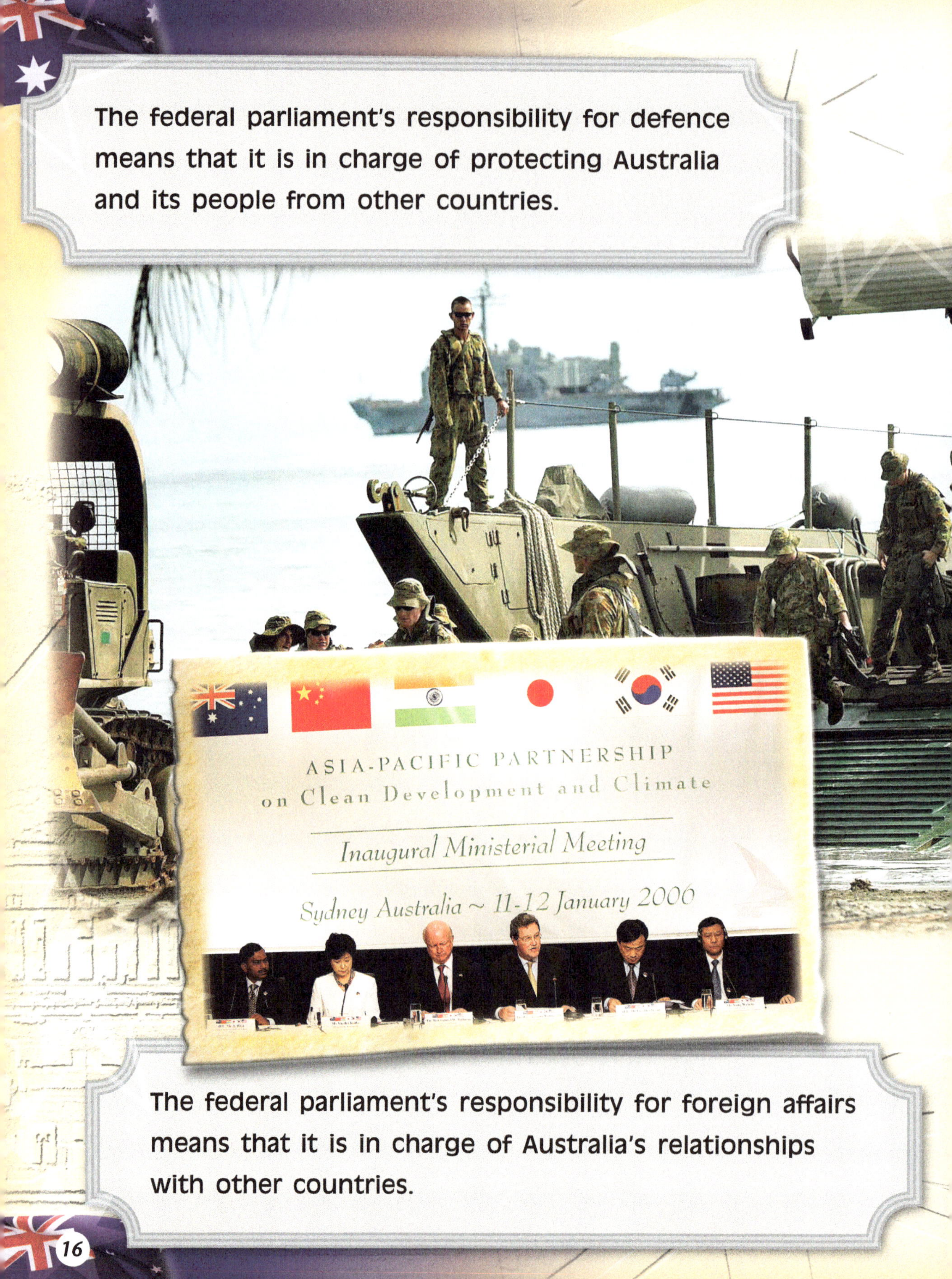

The federal parliament's responsibility for foreign affairs means that it is in charge of Australia's relationships with other countries.

The federal parliament's responsibility
for telecommunications
means that it is in charge of technology
that helps people communicate with each other.

This technology includes
the telephone system,
radio, television
and the Internet.

Chapter 4

STATE AND TERRITORY PARLIAMENTS

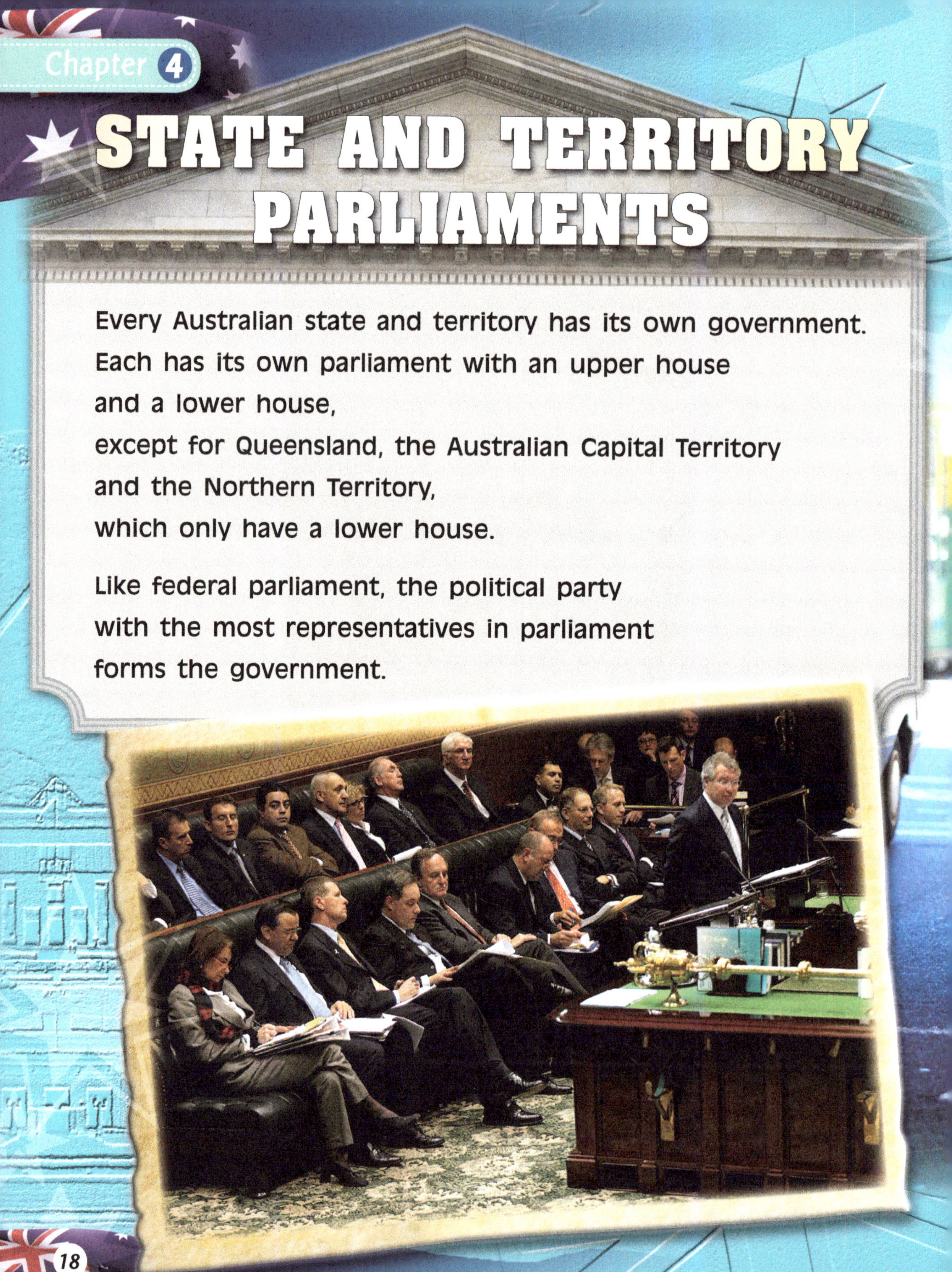

Every Australian state and territory has its own government. Each has its own parliament with an upper house and a lower house, except for Queensland, the Australian Capital Territory and the Northern Territory, which only have a lower house.

Like federal parliament, the political party with the most representatives in parliament forms the government.

The state and territory parliaments are responsible for areas of life that affect people in their state or territory, such as education, emergency services, health and public transport.

The responsibility of state and territory parliaments for education means that they are in charge of schools and what is taught in schools.

Their responsibility for emergency services means that they are in charge of police, ambulance and fire services.

The responsibility of state and territory parliaments for health means that they are in charge of hospitals.

Their responsibility for public transport means that they are in charge of train, tram, bus and ferry services.

LOCAL GOVERNMENTS

Each local government makes laws for a local community, rather than a state or a country.

Local governments are responsible for areas of life that only affect people in that community, such as parking, planning and waste.

The responsibility of local governments for parking means that they decide where and for how long people can park their cars.

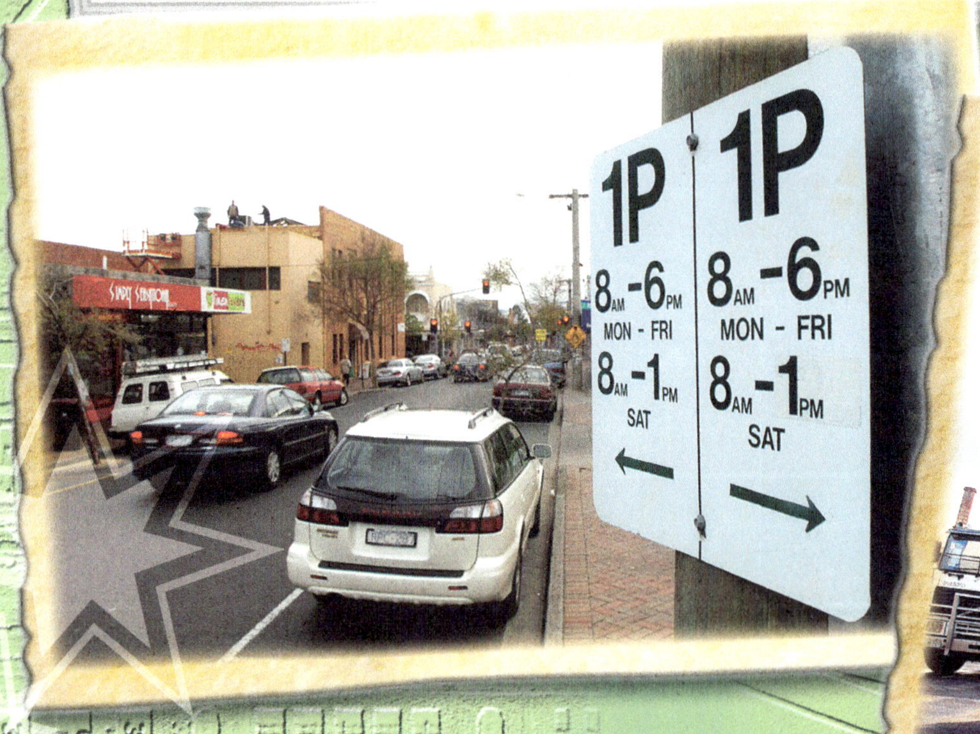

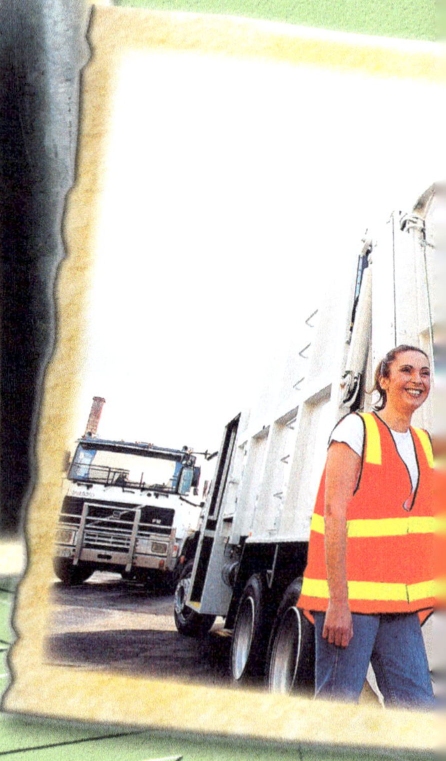

The responsibility of local governments for planning means that they are in charge of building projects in their area.

Their responsibility for waste means that they are in charge of collecting people's rubbish.

Glossary

representatives people who are elected to represent others in parliament

review take another look at something

territory an area in Australia that is not part of a state. The federal government makes the laws for most territories.

Index

customs 14, 15

defence 14, 16

education 19, 20
emergency services 19, 20

federal parliament 7, 10, 12–17, 18
foreign affairs 14, 16

health 19, 21
House of Representatives 12, 13

immigration 14, 15

local government 11, 22–23

parking 22
parliament 6, 7
planning 22, 23
public transport 19, 21

Senate 13
state and territory parliaments 11, 18–21

telecommunications 14, 17

waste 22, 23